When Uncle Took the Fiddle

by **Libba Moore Gray**

illustrated by **Lloyd Bloom**

ORCHARD BOOKS : NEW YORK

Orchard Books, A Grolier Company, 95 Madison Avenue, New York, NY 10016

Manufactured in the United States of America. Printed and bound by Phoenix Color Corp.
The text of this book is set in 17 point Cochin. The illustrations are water-soluble colored pencils on
high-press watercolor paper. 1 2 3 4 5 6 7 8 9 10
Library of Congress Cataloging-in-Publication Data
Gray, Libba Moore. When Uncle took the fiddle / by Libba Moore Gray ; illustrated by Lloyd Bloom.   p.   cm.
Summary: Uncle's inspired playing of the fiddle causes sleepy family members to pick up other instruments and join him,
while the neighbors come to join the celebration.
ISBN 0-531-30137-0 (trade).—ISBN 0-531-33137-7 (lib. bdg.)
[1. Violin—Fiction. 2. Music—Fiction.] I. Bloom, Lloyd, ill. II. Title.
PZ7.G7793Wh 1999   [E]—dc21   98-30239

In memory of Patrick Stacy Fugate and Dorsey Williams, and for
Julie Dye Hensley, Richard Marius, and Lorelle Reeves—L.M.G.

For my father and my mother—L.B.

"Tired," said Grandpa as he settled in his chair.
"Tired," said Grandma as she leaned back in her rocker.

"Tired," said Papa as he flopped onto the sofa.
"Tired," said Mama as she sank down next to Papa.

"Tired," said Brother as he stretched and gave a yawn.
"Tired," said Sister as she put away her book.

"Tired," said Baby as she closed her sleepy eyes.
"Tired," said I as I rubbed the kitten's ear.

Brown Dog heaved a weary sigh and curled up on the rug.

But then . . .
Uncle took the fiddle off the shelf up on the wall.

And when he drew the bow across the silver strings—
    Zee zee

        Saw saw

            Ziggle, ziggle, zang.

How Uncle made that fiddle sing!

Grandpa's feet began to tap.
Grandma's hands began to clap.
Brown Dog lifted floppy ears.

Ziggle, ziggle, zang
Tappity-tap
Clappity-clap.
Brown Dog howled!

Grandma fetched her mouth harp—
Ying-a-yang-a-yoing.

Mama picked her old guitar—
Slide-down-slide.

Brother found some spoons to clack.
Papa strummed a washboard.
Baby held the kitten tight,
while Sister shook some gourds.

Click and clatter
Shu-sha-shu
Rick-a-rack-a-MEW!

The music floated out the door
to folks down in the hollow,
where Homer Jenkins started humming
as he headed up the hill.

Miz Essie followed right behind,
her banjo joining in—

Pick-a-pluck-a-plum
Pick-a-pluck-a-hum.

Custer Crawford brought some cider.
Reuben Reed blew on a jug.
And Lester Chandley entered dancing
like a big old mountain bear.

Step, slide, step.
Turn around.
Whirl around.
Swirl, turn, swirl.

Uncle laughed,
the fiddle flashed,
and Grandpa pulled me up to dance.
Swung me in.
Swung me out.
Spinny, spinny, spin about!

Hands clap.
Toes tap.
In and out.
Spin about!

Pluck-a-pluck-a
    Click and clatter
        Ying-a-yang-a-yoing.

Spin about—
Shu-sha-shu
Rick-a-rack-a-
MEW!

Hands down.
Feet pound.
Round and round.
Faster, faster.
Spin-a-spin-a-spin about!

Hand in hand,
we circled round
until the music
spindled down—
Zing-a-zingle zing.

Neighbors tipped their hats as they headed out the door.

I watched their lanterns wink good-bye.
I waved till they were out of sight.
Brown Dog howled a long good-night.
Kitten mewed and mewed.

Then Uncle and his fiddle played—
one last silver sound.

Shu-sha
 Shu-sha
  Shu.